God Is Near

Jan Jenkins Carter

Illustrated by Nada Serafimovic

God Is Near

Jan Jenkins Carter
Illustrated by Nada Serafimovic

ISBN-13: 978-1537324296

ISBN-10: 1537324292

Edited by Diane Simmons Dill, *Right*Write Productions LLC.
Facebook: https://www.facebook.com/RightwriteProductions.

Formatting and Interior Design by Diane Simmons Dill.

Cover design by Jan Jenkins Carter, Nada Serafimovic, and Diane Simmons Dill.

PRINTED IN THE UNITED STATES OF AMERICA.

Dedication

To Mom, thank you for teaching me to never give up. Your love for the Lord has always challenged me, and your legacy will live on forever in my heart and in the hearts of children everywhere. You are my hero.

To Jack, you believed in me when I didn't believe in myself. Your encouragement brought this book into being. Your love captured my heart over thirty-six years ago and continues to burn bright in my life.

To Coleman, Barrett, and Austin, I believe in you. You will be mighty warriors for Christ, because God has given each of you special talents. May you know that you can do all things, because God Is Near. He has been and always will be. Take hold of His wonderful promise and amazing gift to you.

Down a dusty dirt road, with the moon shining bright, a shooting star caught Annabelle's eye. Lightning bugs twinkled in the night air, and a secret wish began to twinkle deep inside Annabelle's heart.

Annabelle lived with her mom, dad, and three older brothers on a farm in the country. Their small white house was nestled between two large oak trees. The garden was filled with vegetables, blackberries, and Annabelle's all-time favorite, watermelons.

Carlos the cow grazed in the pasture while Pearl the pig rolled in a big mud puddle. Two baby chickens, Giblet and Roo, cheaped and chased Annabelle everywhere she went.

Each morning before school, Annabelle and her brothers fed the animals and gathered the eggs. Then they rode the big yellow school bus to school. Annabelle loved school because she could play with all her friends there.

But church was Annabelle's favorite!

She wanted to hear about God and His love for everyone. She learned that she could talk to God, and He would always listen.

Summer came, and school was out. Annabelle's brothers climbed trees, played ball, and built forts.

But Annabelle played with her dolls and had tea parties...alone. You see, she loved her brothers, but one thing was missing: Annabelle was missing a friend.

One day Annabelle wandered down to a little stream in the woods behind her house. It was a beautiful and peaceful place.

She leaned back on a tree and wiggled her toes in the bubbly water. Feeling all alone, Annabelle began to cry.

"God, I don't have one single friend to play with," she said. "I am sad, and I am lonely. Can you help me?"

A soft voice whispered...
"I am here. You will never be alone again.
You are mine, and I will take care of you."

Annabelle wondered, *who's there?* But she remembered that God always hears our prayers, and she knew God was speaking to her.

Annabelle thought...*if God can make the moon, the stars, and lightning bugs, He can make my secret wish come true and send a friend to me.*

Moments later, a loud chirp echoed from the tree across the stream. Annabelle saw the brightest redbird she had ever seen.

She thought the redbird was a little sign of love God sent just for her.

When Annabelle finished her chores the next day, she could hardly wait to get back to the cool stream.

She sat down, wiggled her toes in the water, and was so surprised at what she saw.

Redbirds covered the tree next to the stream. They were singing a beautiful song to Annabelle.

Annabelle laughed out loud. Her heart was happy and full of joy.

Suddenly, Annabelle felt something gently touch her hand. It was Rigley, a fluffy bunny wearing a big purple bowtie that flopped up and down when he hopped.

He jumped into Annabelle's lap and kissed her on the nose. She was so surprised, it made her giggle. Rigley told Annabelle he was there to be her new best friend. Her secret wish had come true!

Just like Annabelle, Rigley was once sad and
lonely, but then he found God and the redbird.
He hopped up and down with excitement, and
his big purple bowtie flopped in the breeze.

Rigley shared the story his mom told him about the redbird. She said whenever you see a redbird, it means...

God is near!

The redbirds sing God's message of love to anyone who will listen.

The redbird's bright red color reminds us of God's heart of love for us.
He will live in our hearts if we ask him to.

The redbird's chirp is special. When you hear it, it reminds you...God is near.
His redbirds come close when we need them most.

Rigley had met many friends at this very stream. The story of the redbird became true for all of them. Whenever they see a redbird, they know that God is near.

Annabelle giggled again. At that moment, she realized the story of the redbird was true for her, too. She heard God's whisper and then she saw the redbird.

She held Rigley's paws, and they danced 'round and 'round, singing...

"God is near! He is here!"

Annabelle and Rigley looked at the beautiful stream. Suddenly, they heard laughter coming through the woods. The sound came closer and closer, and then happy friends surrounded them.

To their amazement, deer, turtles, raccoons, and foxes had joined them. All the new friends jumped into the cool stream together and began to splash each other. What a sight to see!

From that day on, Annabelle never felt alone again. She felt happy and loved, and so can we, knowing that we are never alone. God is right here, right now.

God is near!

Acknowledgements

I began writing *God Is Near* with one purpose in mind: to share with children that God hears and answers their prayers. He uses signs and wonders to speak to us. I know this is true, because this precious story was planted in my heart as a child by my mom, and it continues to give me hope even today. The story has given so many others hope, as well.

Thank you to my dear friends who now worship with a cloud of witnesses, Brennan Manning and Deacon Bill Steltemeier.

Brennan, in 1994, I was ambushed by you and your loving Abba. A new found grace washed over my soul, one I had never known before. Because of you, I now have many books deep within me, to help carry the message of a loving Father to everyone.

Deacon Bill, I only knew you for a few short years, but your enthusiasm, your intense love for God, and you constantly saying, "live in the present moment," was a life I knew I had to have.

My heartfelt thanks to all the "Dearest Ones" who attend my Bible Study and the rest of my Prayer Warriors. I'm not sure I would be writing this right now, if it weren't for you.

To my endorsers, Dr. Jim Andrews, John Blase, Denise George and Sophie Hudson, thank you so much for believing in me and for your support.

Special thanks to Nada Serafimovic for the beautiful artwork in the book. Her amazing talent brought the story to life in a very special way.

Lastly, to my editor, Diane Simmons Dill. You are a special kiss from the Lord to me. You have been incredibly encouraging, patient, and kind. Your love for me and my dream never wavered. You encouraged me so many late nights when we were working. I can honestly say, I could never have done this without you. There are no words to express my appreciation for you.

A Message From the Author

Thank you for reading my book! My sincere prayer is that you and your child enjoyed reading it and that your child was encouraged by its timeless message. May each precious child who reads the words penned here realize and remember that if they ever feel lonely or discouraged, just remember the redbird and know that God is near! Blessings to each of you.

Jan

Hey, kids! If you enjoyed the storybook version, check out the ebook and coloring book versions on Amazon.com! The coloring book will allow you to color the images with the colors you choose. You can show your own creativity while reading a lovely message that God planted in my heart to share with each of you!

About the Author

Jan Jenkins Carter left the corporate world of marketing and is now a stay-at-home "Registered Mom" who is crazy about her husband, children, family, and friends. But her passions are Jesus and her God-given gift of encouraging others. Whether she's leading a Bible study, writing, speaking or having private lunch meetings with people who need God's embrace, Jan feels it is her honor and privilege to pour God's hope and unconditional love into anyone willing to listen.

A visual learner, Jan is thankful God's Word incorporates illustrations, stories, and word pictures so that we can understand and relate to God. It is with a sense of whimsy, coupled with powerful biblical truths, that Jan penned her first book, *God Is Near*. The book is based on a much-beloved true story passed down for generations within her family. Jan wanted to share the impact the story has had on her own life, such as the simple but profound truths it taught: God is near, He hears and answers our prayers, and He uses signs, wonders, imagination, and miracles to reveal himself to us.

Jan can talk the ears off a billy goat and brings laughter to most situations. She believes that you should worship instead of worry. She enjoys painting, potting flowers, decorating, girl's beach trips, snow skiing, fires in the fireplace, hot buttered popcorn and Raisinets at the movies, her husband's blue eyes and his love for the Lord, holidays with family, the smiles of her children, praise and worship, giving gifts, and the precious sound of her mother's voice.

Jan resides in Birmingham, Alabama with her husband of thirty-six years and her adorable daughter and two sons. She loves life, her family, and her home, and she thinks she has an addiction to Pine-Sol®, Windex®, Pledge®, and Miracle-Gro®!

Made in the USA
Lexington, KY
13 September 2016